HARdCORE
kELLI

WRATH JAMES WHITE

CEMETERY DANCE PUBLICATIONS

Baltimore

❖ 2021 ❖

Trade Paperback Edition   ISBN: 978-1-58767-799-1

Hardcore Kelli

Copyright © 2021 by Wrath James White
Artwork Copyright © 2021 by Chris Odgers
Interior Design © 2021 by Desert Isle Design, LLC

Manufactured in the United States of America.

FIRST TRADE PAPERBACK EDITION

Cemetery Dance Publications
132-B Industry Lane
Unit 7
Forest Hill, MD 21050

Email: info@cemeterydance.con
www.cemeterydance.com

BULLETS WHIZZED PAST Katy as she dashed through the ankle-high, dry and yellowing grass, the knee-high weeds, and the maze of broken recreational vehicles, farm equipment, and other slowly oxidizing junk. She hurdled the rusting skeleton of an old '77 Ford Thunderbird like an Olympic gymnast. Katy had once been a cheerleader, a good one. Once upon a time she could do flips, handsprings, and somersaults with ease. Back in high school she had won cheer competitions with her acrobatics. Her bedroom had been filled with trophies. That was so long ago it felt more like an ancient story from some dusty old history book than something that had actually occurred in her lifetime. Like someone else's life.

She gripped the gleaming battle axe in both hands as she waded through gunfire, determined to reach her archnemesis and end his reign of terror forever. Murder Man stood in the doorway of the rundown mobile home, firing at will. She had found his lair. Now it was time to bring him to justice.

Murder Man's black cowl hid his face in shadow, but she could see the glint of moonlight off the silver battle armor beneath it. He held a gun in each hand, and bullets fed into the pistols from magazines embedded in Murder Man's forearms. Murder Man was a living weapon, half-man, half-machine. He had come to wreak havoc on this innocent little town, the town she grew up in, the town where she'd returned to try to make a new life for herself. She wasn't going to let this evil lunatic destroy her last chance at happiness. Maybe Katy couldn't stop him, but Hardcore Kelli could.

THE WOMAN WAS too fast. For every punch Katy slipped or ducked, two more landed flush on her face. She could barely see out of her right eye. Her opponent's jab had raised a huge hematoma above and beneath her eye, swelling it shut. A cut above Katy's left eyebrow was dripping onto her face, into her eye. Katy was almost completely blind, but she wasn't giving up. Katy was tough. Her opponent was a better boxer than she was, so Katy had to turn it into a dog fight, a test of wills. She had to make it an ugly, brutal war.

Sheer stubborn grit and intestinal fortitude had carried her through hard fights before. It was just a numbers game, a matter of returning fire, landing two or three shots for every shot landed on her. It didn't matter that she could barely see. She could feel. As long as the woman was hitting her, then Katy knew exactly where she was. One thing she knew for certain was that you couldn't throw a punch with your right hand and block with your right at the same time. Every time Tatianna Simms threw that right cross, she would be open for the left hook, and, eventually, Katy was certain she'd be able to land the punch that would knock that slick bitch on her fancy ass.

"You've got to bring ass to get ass," her trainer would say. Katy had no problem taking a punch to give a punch. She'd been through wars before.

The problem was she was now taking two or three shots to land one, and that just wasn't good math. She felt a punch land right below her rib cage. She didn't see it land but knew from the force of the blow that it had been another right hand. That meant Tatianna's right cheek would be exposed. Katy threw a hard left hook and felt the jolt of the punch travel down her arm into her shoulders when she landed on the woman's cheek. It was the punch Katy'd been trying to land the entire fight, her homerun, the one that should have won her the fight. But Tatianna was still standing. She hadn't even wobbled. Katy felt that familiar self-doubt creep inside her brain and take up residency.

I'm going to lose. I'm going to lose again.

Tatianna was a lightning-fast, skillful boxer, with more than sixty amateur fights under her belt, including a National Golden Gloves title and a stint as an alternate on the women's U.S. Olympic Boxing Team. Katy was your garden variety brawler. She'd turned pro after only eight amateur fights, because she needed the money, then she'd been given a shot at the world title after eleven pro bouts. She'd lost that fight and followed it by losing two of her last three matches. Her promoter told her she would be cut from the promotion if she lost this fight. Her trainer had begun hinting that she should retire if she lost another fight. But Katy was only twenty-nine. She was much too young to think about retirement.

Katy managed to slip her opponent's jab and land a hard left hook to Tatianna's liver, then followed it up with an overhand right that caught Tatianna just above the ear and drove her back into the ropes. Hope swelled in Katy's bosom as she closed in for the kill. She'd been here many times before, with a hurt opponent pinned against the ropes. Katy was an excellent finisher—calm, patient, but ferocious, not wasting any shots, making every punch count. But this time as she closed in on her opponent, landing a jab to the stomach and another one to the forehead that whipped Tatianna's head back, preparing to unleash a barrage of right and left hooks, she caught a glimpse of Tatianna's face. She wasn't hurt. The punch might have knocked her off balance, but it hadn't stunned or staggered her.

When Katy closed in, her punches hit nothing but air as Tatianna slipped under the left hook, spun off the ropes, and was gone. What followed were three more rounds of Katy eating jabs and right hands as she chased Tatianna around the ring, trying unsuccessfully to corner her against the ropes so she could land something significant. The bell rang, and Katy staggered back to her corner, tired, bleeding, swollen, and utterly dejected.

"You've got to show me something or I'm stopping this fight. You've only got three more rounds. Do you want to win this fight?" her trainer, Tito "Taco" Sandavol, asked.

Katy just stared at him. She knew he wouldn't really throw in the towel. He'd let her die out there in the middle of the ring before giving up on one of his fighters. Taco's faith in the boxers he trained was both empowering and terrifying. How much punishment would she have to take before he was satisfied that she couldn't win this?

"Are you going to go out there and fight or not? I need three more hard rounds out of you. These last three rounds could change your whole life!"

Three rounds. Nine minutes. Five hundred and forty seconds. It sounds like nothing—when you're outside the ring. But from where Katy was sitting, it sounded like an eternity. The average street fight lasts only eight seconds. People died in street fights. She would have to endure the equivalent of sixty-seven of them. She'd read somewhere that it took ten seconds for a body to hit the ground after falling from the top of the Empire State Building. She remembered counting to ten, imagining how much time you would have to look around, see the buildings rush by, the ground rushing up to greet you, to contemplate your entire life, the moment of impact, to regret. Three rounds. Five hundred and forty seconds. Like falling from the top of the Empire State Building fifty-four times.

"You gonna give me everything you got left in you, mija? Or you gonna let that bitch keep whooping on you? Do you want to be champion? You want a chance to fight for the title again or no?"

Katy didn't know how to answer. Did she want to win? No one seemed to care about her anymore. Now that she was no longer the hot new prospect tearing through the ranks like a weed whacker, half the people she'd once called her friends had abandoned her. Everyone had written her off. As much as she wanted to show them all that she still had the strength, the will, the talent to be a world champion, she had begun to doubt whether she really did.

HARDCORE KELLI

As the fight doctor shined a penlight into her eyes, asking her how many fingers he was holding up, and her cut man slathered Vaseline and adrenaline into the huge gash over her eye while mashing an enswell into her other swollen eye, Taco tapped the back of her neck three times. He knew she couldn't see and was telling her how many fingers the doctor was holding up so he didn't stop the fight. He knew she couldn't see, but he was willing to send her back out there to eat more punches, get her face even more disfigured, her brains scrambled, probably another concussion, and another step closer to pugilistic dementia. She had already started hearing things, seeing things. People thought it was because of the drugs. She'd been taking lots of painkillers lately. But the pills weren't the cause of the hallucinations, they were the only thing that kept them at bay.

"One," she said. Taco tapped the back of her neck three times again, but Katy repeated, "One."

The doctor turned to the referee and waved off the fight. And Taco knew what she had done.

"You quit," Taco hissed. "I can't believe you just quit. My fighters don't quit! Not ever!"

"Fuck you, Taco," Katy replied.

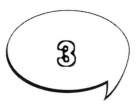

THE POST-FIGHT CONFERENCE was hell. Katy's right eye was still swollen shut. A thick wad of gauze and tape covered her left eyebrow. Livid red, blue, and purple bruises festooned what had once been a reasonably attractive face. She could only imagine how bad she looked on camera. She supposed she would have made a good extra in a zombie movie at that moment. She would not have needed any special-effects makeup. Katy already looked like the walking dead. But the worse thing was that Taco, her long-time trainer, wasn't there. They'd had a blow-up in the dressing room, and he'd walked out, refusing to ever train her again.

"My fighters don't quit!" Taco yelled at her, throwing his towel across the locker room, tossing his cornerman's bucket to the floor, spilling its contents everywhere, before kicking over a trashcan. Katy had witnessed many of his tantrums over the years. She was immune to them now.

"I couldn't fucking see! You were going to send me back out there to let that woman beat my head in!"

"Oh, bullshit, mija! Tatianna can't crack a fucking egg! Everyone in boxing knows that. All her KOs were against tomato cans. She couldn't hurt you. You've been hit harder by better. You were scared. You've lost your heart, mija!"

His words stung. Katy's heart, her strength and courage, were all she had in this world, what she relied on to get her from one trial, tragedy, or disappointment to the next. If her trainer was right, and she'd finally lost even that, then she was truly fucked.

"I ain't your fucking mija," Katy snarled. She stood up, standing nose to nose with her trainer, scowling menacingly.

"Oh, you want to get tough with me now, but you just rolled over for Tatianna? Where was this badass out there in the ring?"

Katy balled up her fist and punched the locker to the left of Taco's head, leaving a disappointingly minute dent.

"I did everything I fucking could! She was faster than me! Better than me! I couldn't even hurt her!"

Taco shook his head, refusing to listen. "You didn't do everything! You quit!" He jabbed a finger at her, aiming it like a gun.

Katy wondered for a moment, if it had been a gun, in his anger, would he have pulled the trigger? Would she have wanted him to? She could see herself challenging him to do it, begging him to put her out of her misery.

Taco lowered his hand and shoved it into his pocket. He continued, this time in a calmer voice, the voice he always used when he was trying to explain something to her that he felt should have been obvious. Katy hated that condescending tone. She much preferred when he yelled.

"You have one of the best left hooks in all of boxing, male or female. Mike Tyson wishes he had a hook like yours. No bullshit. As long as you're in there throwing shots, giving it your all, you've always got a puncher's chance."

Katy scoffed. "A puncher's chance? That's what people say when they know you have no fucking chance in hell."

"You could have at least finished the fight."

"For what, Taco? I was going to lose anyway. You didn't even want me to take this fight."

"And I was right, too."

"Oh, fuck you, Taco."

"You don't get to call me Taco anymore. Only my friends call me Taco. You…you let me down. You made a fool of me out there. You broke my heart."

He walked out of her dressing room.

Katy stared out across the anemic smattering of reporters. There had been ten times this many reporters when she was the top contender, in line for a title shot. But now she was just yesterday's news, a car wreck to intrigue those with a morbid curiosity for such things, a cautionary tale trainers would tell their young fighters.

"Will you retire now?" asked a skinny black reporter, wearing a red and white polka dot bowtie.

"I don't know. Maybe."

Another reporter, an old gray-haired guy from one of the few remaining boxing magazines, raised his hand. He'd been chronicling the sport since Muhammed Ali won his first world title and still wrote about the fight game in poetic flourishes, like he was describing man's noblest endeavor rather than a brutal blood sport that left most of its participants with permanent brain damage.

"Katy, following your last two losses, you admitted to having a drug and alcohol problem and blamed those losses on a lack of discipline and focus. Recently, you were arrested in Vegas on a DUI, and police reports said you were hallucinating and babbling incoherently about monsters. You never went into drug rehabilitation following these events. Did any of that play a role in your loss here tonight, and will you go into rehab now?"

Katy looked around for her trainer. This is when he would have normally jumped in with a funny story to break the tension, change the subject, and usually insult her opponent, or question the competency of the judges or referee. But he was gone. He'd abandoned her just like everyone else.

"No comment," Katy said and then walked off the podium.

"**GET THE FUCK** off me! I'll fucking kill you!" Katy woke up swinging. Her hands were balled into tight fists, and she was yelling, breathing hard, throwing punches in the darkness at an attacker who wasn't there, who hadn't been there in years. She looked around the room, squinting through the veil of night. The glow from the streetlights outside cast shadows around the tiny studio apartment, and she scrutinized each one for a possible threat. She saw something move. A rush of adrenaline flooded her system. Her muscles tensed and hairs rose on her neck.

"Come on, motherfucker!"

One of the shadows seemed to take on the shape of a man, a big man. Katy leapt from her bed and charged the figure, determined to destroy the intruder before he could hurt her again. Before he could victimize her again. Before he could make her hate herself again.

"Leave me the fuck alone!"

Katy grit her teeth and swung a haymaker at the shadowman's head. Her fists sailed harmlessly through the dark. Just a shadow. No intruder. No boogie man. Just a nightmare. A hallucination.

"You're trippin'. Get yourself together, girl," Katy whispered, rubbing her palms down her face.

She could still smell the distant odor of sweat, beer, cheap cologne, and cigarettes from years ago. She could taste it, as if she'd brought a piece of that rapist piece of shit with her out of her nightmares. She couldn't remember exactly which rapist piece of shit it was this time. Her piece of shit ex-husband, or the piece of shit jock who'd molested her in high school. They both blended together in her dreams into one big, monumental, rapist asshole.

Katy stood and staggered into the bathroom. A bottle of Wild Turkey and a couple of Oxycontin waited to wash the taste of fear and shame from her mouth and help her fall back to sleep. This time, hopefully, a dreamless one. Tomorrow she would be working the day shift at the Jiggle Joint. If she wanted to make any money at all, she would need to at least appear enthusiastic about shaking her ass for the losers who patronized the place, and she needed to be well rested to do that.

"DIDN'T YOU USED to be a boxer? One of them other girls said you was a fighter. I think I seen you on TV once."

Katy sighed. Those jealous bitches knew she didn't like talking about her past, especially her boxing career, and definitely not with customers. They all hated her because she was one of the only girls at the club who refused to fuck the customers. They thought it meant she believed she was better than them. And she did. They were all just a bunch of sluts and skanks as far as she was concerned.

"You must have me confused with someone else," Katy said as she wiggled her ass inches from his face. "My name is Sapphire."

"Well, Sapphire, you're definitely a knockout, even if you won't admit to being a fighter. Damn shame too. I'd have paid double for a blowjob from a former world champion."

Katy sighed and rolled her eyes. She hated these fat, sexist, overprivileged businessmen who came into the club thinking every stripper was a whore. Every one of them had a wife at home waiting for them, not suspecting their hubby was out somewhere paying strippers to get their dicks wet.

"Well, sorry to disappoint you, but I never won a world title. I lost. And I don't give blowjobs, only hand jobs. And yeah, that'll cost you double."

"I knew it. I recognized you right off. I saw your title fight. Man, you really took a beating."

"A hundred and fifty dollars."

"What?"

"You want me to jack you off? That'll be a hundred and fifty dollars, or you can just keep staring at my ass for the rest of this song and then go find some other girl to get you off."

"But that's more than double," he said.

Katy found the expression of incredulity and outrage on his face comical. This middle-aged walrus of a man, stuffed into a business suit that probably cost what Katy took home in a month, was genuinely offended that he would have to pay more to sexually exploit some poor, less-fortunate woman. She had no sympathy for him.

Katy turned around and folded her arms across her chest. She still worked out every day, so her arms and shoulders were muscular. She still looked like a fighter.

"I don't like reminiscing about my boxing career. So if I have to listen to you go on about it, that's going to cost you more."

The walrus began to laugh. "Okay, fair enough. But how about I give you two hundred, and you tell me about it?"

"Tell you about what?"

"Your fights. How you beat those bitches down."

Katy smiled and shook her head. This guy was a genuine piece of work. "You want me to talk about fighting while I jack you off?"

The walrus nodded. A lecherous grin spread across his face. "Make it three hundred."

"Three hundred? Why three hundred?"

Katy rubbed a hand between his legs, stroking his modest erection through his cotton twill slacks.

"Because fuck you. That's why."

The walrus pulled out three crisp hundred dollar bills he'd probably withdrawn from the ATM for just this purpose. He stuffed them into her G-string while licking his lips. Katy grabbed him by the jaw, barely stifling her original impulse to punch him in the mouth.

"What do you want to hear?"

"Tell me what it feels like to beat up a woman," the walrus said, unbuckling his pants and unzipping his fly. He wasn't wearing underwear. He probably thought he was clever for that, like he was the first guy to think of going commando at a strip club to make it easier for a dancer to give him a glitter-dusted rub and tug. His little pink erection popped out like a prairie dog from its den.

Katy's stomach tightened and bile rose in her throat. "Why? Why do you want to hear me talk about fighting?"

"I just want to know what it feels like to hurt one of those mean-ass bitches."

Katy scowled. "Does this have anything to do with the mean-ass bitch you go home to every night? Or was it the mean-ass bitch that raised you?"

The walrus smiled, taking Katy's hand and guiding it to his cock, where she began to stroke.

"Both."

This is the last time. I'm not doing this anymore, Katy thought. But she'd had similar thoughts before and always wound up right back here.

Katy was lost in her thoughts, stroking and tugging on the walrus's little penis, trying to ignore his growing tusks and whiskers when she felt his thick stubby fingers attempting to ease their way inside her.

"What the fuck?!"

The first punch was an accident, instinctual. She'd been startled and had merely lashed out without thinking. He definitely deserved it though.

"Shit! Why'd you hit me?"

"You don't fucking touch me!"

"Oh, come on. What's the big deal? I'm paying you, aren't I?"

The next thirty punches were deliberate. When Katy finally stopped pounding her fists into the walrus's face, and he slipped to the floor, bleeding and unconscious, she had already decided that this was her last night as a dancer at the Jiggle Joint.

Katy reached into the walrus's pants pocket and removed his wallet.

"Me too, motherfucker," Katy hissed through clenched teeth.

She took another three hundred and then walked out of the VIP room and into the dancers' dressing room, where she snatched up her clothes and purse and left. But it hadn't ended there.

They say bad news and bad times come in threes. In Katy's experience, it came in great heaping piles. Trouble sought itself.

HARDCORE KELLI

Violence didn't just beget violence, it attracted it like a beacon. She'd read once about a woman who'd been raped and dumped by the side of a freeway. When she waved down a car, looking for someone to help her, she was raped again by the driver of the first vehicle that stopped for her. This didn't surprise Katy at all. Predators sought the weakest animals, and an animal that had already been attacked and wounded by another predator was an enticement that brought out the prey drive in this planet's more despicable denizens. So when Katy saw the shadow creep up from behind her, she wasn't surprised.

Getting approached by creepy fucks in the parking lot was a regular occurrence. Usually, Katy waited for one of the bouncers to walk her to her car for just this reason. But after kicking the shit out of one of the club's wealthier patrons, she hadn't thought it wise to ask any favors of the club. She had just wanted to get the hell out of there. In retrospect, it hadn't been smart of her. Trouble comes in great big, heaping, steaming piles. Katy balled her hands into fists as the shadow drew closer, so close she could feel the man's breath on the back of her neck.

Katy's hands were bruised and swollen. The skin on her knuckles was ripped, and her right hand felt like something was broken inside, but Katy wasn't in the mood for any more shit. If some dirt bag was going to try attacking her, she wasn't going to talk her way out of it. She wasn't even going to try.

The guy was a regular. A construction worker who usually staggered in every Friday after cashing his check, still wearing his work clothes and muddy boots, stinking of nine or ten hours of relentless sweating. He had that hard, wiry muscle you get from long hours of manual labor rather than hours in an air-conditioned gym. She didn't know his name. She couldn't remember it no matter how many times he'd told it to her. It was something Spanish sounding, so she assumed he was part Mexican even though he just looked like your average blue-collar redneck to her.

He'd been at the club earlier, before her little incident with the walrus asshole. As had become their ritual, Katy had waited until he'd downed a few Coronas before knocking back a shot of whiskey herself and walking over to his table.

"Wanna lap dance?" she asked him. He nodded, patting his lap and simultaneously signaling the cocktail waitress for another Corona and his third or fourth shot of tequila. Usually he had two or three lap dances, and five or six beers, before stumbling out the door to wherever rat hole he called home. This time he kept her on his lap for more than an hour, buying one lap dance after another and chasing each one with a shot of tequila. When he started getting handsy, Katy signaled the bouncer and had him removed. That was how her shift had begun a few hours ago. She should have known it was only going to get worse from there.

She hated doing it. If he had just asked (and paid for the privilege), she would have happily jacked him off in the VIP room. What Katy did not like was being manhandled by anyone. She'd gone through enough of that in her marriage. So when the guy began pawing at her breasts, she'd had him kicked out. Obviously, the guy was having a bad night. But that wasn't her problem.

She recognized the overpowering stench of sweat and beer right away. There was no doubting who it was. He kept one hand over her mouth and groped for her breast with the other. That gave Katy enough room to crack him in the ribs with an elbow. She whipped her head back and felt the satisfying crunch of her skull connecting with cartilage, and the sudden splash of blood down the back of her neck as her head crushed the guy's nose. He grunted and removed his hand from her mouth, and Katy turned and hit him with a jab, right cross, left hook, right uppercut combination that sent him crashing to the sidewalk where he struck his head on the concrete parking curb. He died almost instantly. Katy watched his eyes fix in place, staring at something beyond this world, beyond this life, as his breathing stopped and his body twitched a few times before lying still. That's when Katy decided to go home. All the way home. Back to the little town of dirt farmers and oil workers she'd grown up in. Back to her mother's house.

THE CROWDED GREYHOUND whipped into the bus depot, brakes squealing, belching black exhaust fumes. Katy let out a sigh. The last time she'd seen this place, she'd been going the opposite direction, leaving the small town in which she'd spent the first nineteen years of her life, determined to never come back. But now her fortunes had changed, and she had nowhere else to go.

Katy hadn't told anyone she was coming, so no one waited to greet her as she stepped off the bus. Moving back home with her mom at age twenty-nine was the last and most demoralizing blow in a succession of humiliations that began when she had an abortion at fifteen and then ran away and eloped with the jerk who'd knocked her up a year later. Taking up boxing had been part of the personal rehabilitation that had given her the strength and confidence to walk away from that abusive asshole. She'd left that jerk right before her first amateur fight, minus a couple teeth. In hindsight, she should have moved back home then. It would have saved her many years of painful memories and regret.

Katy carried her backpack containing her underwear, makeup, toiletries, phone charger, jewelry, and laptop and waited for the driver to unload the rest of the luggage from the bus's cargo hold. A large duffel bag held everything else she owned. Mostly just clothes. She slung the bag over her shoulder and walked through the bus depot and onto Main Street. The town hadn't changed much at all, except there was now a Domino's Pizza and a Starbucks. Everything else—Corky's Diner, Maude's Odds and Ends, Smith's Feed and Hardware Store, The Saloon—was exactly the same. Katy considered walking down the street to The Saloon to get a drink to steel her nerves before going home. But having just one drink wasn't how Katy was wired, and showing up drunk at her mother's front door after eleven years probably wouldn't be smart.

There was a toy store across the street from the bus depot that also sold kids clothes. Some of Katy's fondest memories were of her mother taking her there to pick out a toy with the money her grandfather always gave her for her birthday. Her grandfather always gave her five dollars, and Mother would make her promise to only pick something that cost five dollars or less. Katy never could, and her mom would always end up making up the difference. Katy smiled.

She walked up the street toward the old Wallace Ranch. The weight of her luggage made her lean to one side, and her duffel bag bumped against her thigh, making her lurch and stumble as she made her way down the sidewalk. It was going to be a long walk home.

HARDCORE KELLI

The Wallace Ranch had once been a huge two hundred-acre cattle ranch and corn and sorghum farm, but more than half the land had been sold off bit by bit to smaller farmers, a trailer park, and a large entry-level housing development. In Katy's mind, it was all still just the Wallace Ranch and forever would be.

Next to it stood the high school Katy was supposed to graduate from. It was a small school with a disproportionately huge football stadium. Everyone in town watched the high school football games on Friday nights. The football players, in this town, were like rock stars. Beyond the school, and the farms, were old rundown houses, and trailers on ten or twenty acres of land with cows and chickens or corn or soy growing on it. And beyond that was the old master planned community of cheap little cookie cutter houses on quarter acre lots that had once been part of the Wallace Ranch. That's where Katy had grown up. The houses had all been brand new, some still under construction, when Katy was in high school. Now they looked only slightly better than the old mobile and modular homes rotting on the acres of farmland she'd passed on her way in from town.

Just on the outskirts of town was the oil refinery that belched noxious chemicals into the air and polluted the soil. Most of the people in town who didn't work for the Wallaces, or run their own businesses, worked at the oil refinery. That's why they ignored the town's unusually high instances of cancer, asthma, emphysema, and mental and physical birth defects. It didn't take a genius to connect the black cloud of fumes that drifted over the town from the refinery's smokestacks to the fact that conjoined twins occurred more in this town than anywhere else in the world. But no one wanted to see the refinery close down.

If it went away, so would the town itself. And despite its ills, this was the only place Katy thought of as home, and it always would be.

In her heart, Katy was still a small-town girl. The big cities had almost destroyed her. Going back to her roots was what she needed to revitalize and regroup. At least that was the magic she was searching for. She didn't know if she'd stay in this town forever. That all depended on how her mom reacted to her return. How the entire town reacted.

Katy stood on her mom's front porch with everything she owned packed into a backpack and large duffel bag, ringing the doorbell, and dreading the reunion. All she could think about was that construction worker's eyes rolling up in his head and his breath hissing out in one long sigh before his breathing stopped forever. She kept wondering if she should have called an ambulance or tried to administer CPR. But then she'd picture herself being hauled away in handcuffs and tossed into a cell. She'd heard of people being locked up for years waiting on trials. She'd even heard of a guy who'd been forgotten. He'd sat in prison for six years, some of that time in solitary confinement, without a trial, on a minor marijuana possession charge, before anyone remembered to look at his file. The thought of being locked up for years made Katy's breath feel constricted, like she was being suffocated.

She had done nothing wrong. She had killed an asshole in self-defense. Still, she knew she should have stayed and told her story to the police. But instead, she'd run. And coupled with her assault of the walrus in the business suit, that made her look guilty as hell. Most people didn't even believe you could sexually harass a stripper, or even rape one. They looked at sexual assault as part of the job description for an adult entertainer. If she had stayed, it would have been the word of a stripper with a history of violence, mental illness, and substance abuse, versus that guy's grieving family. She hadn't liked those odds.

When her mother opened the door, the old woman's eyes widened and a trembling smile burst onto her face. She gathered Katy into her arms, told her she loved her, and then wept on Katy's shoulder, kissing her face repeatedly.

Katy was stunned. Of all the receptions she'd envisioned, this had not been one of them.

"Oh, my baby! You're back! I knew you'd come home someday. I just knew you'd come home. I missed you so much."

No questions. No angry accusations or recriminations. Just a big, warm, teary-eyed welcome. It was more than Katy had expected or felt she deserved. Her mother welcoming her back without an argument or even an "I told you so" was worse than if the old woman had yelled and cussed at her. She had always imagined coming home wealthy and famous, proving wrong everyone who thought she'd never amount to anything. But a manager who was too eager to capitalize on her good looks, pushing her into a title fight after only eleven professional bouts, had dashed those dreams when she was outclassed, outpointed, and eventually knocked out in the fifth round.

Seeing just how much she had been hurting the woman who'd given her birth with her absence and silence all these years, Katy felt wretched. She wondered if her mother, or the little sister who had been an infant when Katy left home, would have welcomed her back so easily if they knew half of what she'd been doing the last eleven years. If they knew that she was a murderer.

"Where have you been all these years?"

Katy shook her head and continued to weep.

"**COME ON, MOTHERFUCKER!** Come on! I'll fucking kill you! I'll fucking kill you!" Katy woke up yelling curses and throwing punches again. She was covered in sweat, and her hands were balled into tight fists as she swung at the empty air. Her teeth were clenched, mouth twisted into a snarl, panting like she was in the ring again, rather than on a hide-a-bed couch in her mother's living room.

"What's going on? Katy?" Her mother rushed into the room, snapping on the lights, flooding the room with sudden, harsh illumination as she raced to Katy's bedside.

Katy winced from the intrusion, and her snarl deepened. "I'm okay, Mom. Just a bad dream," Katy said, shielding her eyes from the light.

Her mother's brow furrowed in concern. "It sounded like you were fighting someone in here."

"Just a dream. Can you turn off the light, Mom? You're blinding me."

Katy's mother walked back across the room to flick off the light switch and then returned to sit beside Katy. "You know, you used to have really vivid dreams when you were a kid. Night terrors. You would wake up screaming, fighting. Sometimes I'd find you running through the house, or hiding in a closet or under a bed. It used to scare the hell out of me."

Katy's mother rubbed her forehead. Her hand was so soft and warm. Katy felt like she could just melt right into it. Her mother had always known exactly how to soothe her. Katy sat up and leaned into her mother, who wrapped her arms around her and began to rock slowly.

"I sort of remember that a little," Katy said. "I don't remember what the dreams were about though."

"You would say the monsters were coming, or the bad people were trying to get you. I found you outside my door one night, holding a knife. You said you were going to protect me from the monsters. That's when I took you to a doctor, but they just wanted to give you drugs. I did what they said for a while, but I didn't like how drowsy it made you in the morning. You'd walk around like a zombie all day. So I stopped giving you the pills, and your nightmares got worse. But then you just grew out of it. Or at least I thought you did."

Katy hadn't outgrown the dreams. They had come with less frequency as she had gotten older, but they still came. And she remembered every one of them. The dark, shadowy men with no faces who came to kill her and her family. Sometimes, she saw them even when she was awake. Occasionally, in her dreams, the dark men wore faces of people she knew. Friends, acquaintances, even family members. Following one of those dreams, it would be weeks before she could stand being around those people again, before she could trust them.

The drugs had helped. Percocets. Dilaudid. Fentanyl. Opioids that, along with copious amounts of alcohol, would numb everything and make her sleep dreamless. But they had also probably ruined her fighting career. She had gone to a psychiatrist a couple months ago, who'd prescribed an antipsychotic called clozapine. Katy had filled the prescription but had never taken any. For some reason the idea of taking antipsychotic medication scared her worse than the dreams themselves. It would mean admitting that she was crazy. She wasn't quite ready to do that. But she had stayed away from painkillers. She hadn't taken anything in weeks. Now, the nightmares were back.

Katy forced a smile and nodded.

"I have outgrown them. It's just probably being back in this house. It's still strange for me. I'm sure that's all."

Her mother smiled a crooked, worried smile that trembled hesitantly across her face. She kissed Katy on the forehead and then continued to rock her like an infant until Katy fell back to sleep.

"COME TRICK OR treating with me tomorrow! It'll be fun!"

Katy didn't share her little sister's enthusiasm for the holiday. She didn't share her little sister's enthusiasm for anything these days. The girl was a bouncing, smiling, giggling ball of glittering optimism, whereas Katy struggled to find a compelling argument for taking the next breath.

"Please? Please come with me," her little sister whined.

"I don't think so, kiddo. I'm not really the trick or treating type. You're a big girl now. You can go by yourself. Go with your friends or something."

Samantha was twelve years old now, and Katy knew almost nothing about her younger sister. She looked so much like Katy, but it was an opposite yin-yang image. Whereas Katy had been a depressed and sullen child, Samantha was practically bubbly. She had an infectious smile complete with deep dimples. Katy almost resented the kid's optimism and—cuteness. She would get whatever she wanted in life with that smile. Doors would open for her wherever she went, just because she was pretty, well, honestly, beautiful. Katy wasn't ugly either. She knew that. But she was more sexy than pretty. Her beauty was of the "bad girl" variety.

"I can't go by myself. Kids've gotten attacked around here."

"Attacked? What attacks?"

"The teacher said a couple girls got attacked walking home from school. One happened last week and another one happened just yesterday. I saw it on the news too. They said the guy who attacked them did stuff to 'em. Messed 'em up bad."

Katy had been web-surfing on her phone, but what Samantha said made her put her phone down and give full attention to her baby sister. *Did stuff to 'em.* She knew what that meant. They didn't live in the best neighborhood. Muggings, robberies, even rapes and homicides were not uncommon. But child molestation was something new, and Samantha was a cute kid. Katy knew she'd never forgive herself if some pervert attacked her baby sister just because she was too lazy to take the kid trick or treating.

"Okay, kiddo. I'll take you, but I ain't wearing no costume."

Samantha clasped her hands in front of her face as if she were preparing to recite a prayer. "Pleeeeeeeassse! You have to!"

"I wouldn't even know what to wear. I ain't going as no sexy witch or vampiress or anything stupid like that. I do have some pride left."

"You could go as Catwoman or Super Girl. Ooooh! I know! You should go as Hardcore Kelli!"

"Who?"

"Hardcore Kelli. She's a badass. She's a vigilante who kills criminals that hurt women and kids and stuff. She carries a big hatchet. It's like this giant battle-axe. She chops the criminals' heads off!"

"So she's like a serial killer?"

Samantha frowned. "No. She's a good guy. She's a hero—a superhero."

"A hero that chops off people's heads? Sounds like a psycho to me. Only crazy people chop other people up with axes. I thought superheroes weren't supposed to kill people?"

Samantha smirked and shook her head. "That's old comics. That comic code stuff. Nobody follows that anymore, not even the big two."

"The big two?"

"Duh. Marvel and D.C."

"Oh. So what does she look like?"

"I'll show you," Samantha said, running across the room to her closet. She removed a couple of shoe boxes and began rummaging through them.

"What's her name again?" Katy asked.

"Hardcore Kelli."

"Sounds like a porn name."

"A what?"

"Never mind."

Samantha pulled a comic book from one of the boxes. It was wrapped in a plastic sleeve and Samantha handled it delicately, as if it were something rare and valuable.

"You can't touch it. You can only look at it, okay?"

Katy rolled her eyes. "Okay."

Samantha pointed to a goth chick on the cover who was carrying a comically oversized battle-axe. Even with the character's Amazonian physique, it should have been impossible for her to swing the thing more than a few times without exhausting herself.

Hardcore Kelli had black hair separated into two ponytails, and pale bloodless skin, black eyeliner and eye shadow, black lipstick and nail polish, like every Depeche Mode and Marilyn Manson fan Katy had known in high school. She wore torn, black, fishnet stockings beneath cut off black mini-shorts. She sported black combat boots that came almost up to her knees. She had a torn black T-shirt with a white smiley face on it, only the face was snarling angrily rather than smiling. The woman looked like some sort of angry goth clown. Despite Katy's cynicism, she had to admit, Hardcore Kelli did look pretty badass.

"So what's her superpower? What does she do?"

"She kicks ass!"

"Watch your mouth," Katy said.

Samantha frowned. "Whatever."

"Okay, so how exactly does she kick ass? I mean, besides the fact that she carries a big-ass axe? How does she keep from getting shot or jumped by a whole bunch of dudes?"

"She can take a lot of punishment. She heals up real fast."

"Like Wolverine?"

"Not that fast. Just faster than most people. She used to be a boxer, just like you. That's why she's got muscle. But she had this sleazy trainer that slipped her some experimental steroid and mixed it with cocaine or meth or something. She wound up killing her opponent in the ring and had to go into hiding. That's when her other powers started coming out. Her healing ability. "

"Is that it? I mean, how did super healing ability make her kill her opponent in the ring? Did it give her like super strength or something?"

"Kinda. She has these roid rages where she gets really strong and vicious. Not Superman or Hulk strong. More like somewhere between Captain America and Batman. But the healing ability and her viciousness is her real power. No matter what you do to her, she just keeps coming. She always keeps coming. She turns into like a beast when she's angry. I mean, not literally. She just gets real mean. That's when you know heads are about to roll. And when she's like that, pain doesn't bother her. She just keeps coming. She sort of likes the pain. Sometimes she just lets the bad guys beat on her until they tire themselves out, then she kicks their asses."

"Like the rope-a-dope?"

"The what?"

"Mohammed Ali versus George Foreman? Rumble in the Jungle?"

Samantha shrugged. "The grill guy?"

"Well, before he was the grill guy, George Foreman was this big, strong, mean guy who knocked dudes out with one punch. And Ali was an older, smaller guy, but he was fast and slick. When they fought, Ali leaned against the ropes and let Big George hit him until Foreman got tired. Then Ali came off the ropes and knocked Big George out!"

Katy frowned. She was staring at Samantha, brow furrowed in concern.

"I guess that does sound like me. How did you know I used to box?"

Samantha smiled. "Everyone around here knows! We all watched your fights on TV. Mom was so proud of you, but she couldn't stand watching you get beaten up. She had to leave the room."

Katy shook her head and let out a long sigh.

"Great. And here I was worried about them finding out I was a stripper."

"You were a stripper?"

"Never mind."

"So? Will you do it?"

Katy smiled and nodded. "Yeah. I guess so. I think I have everything for the costume except the shirt—and that big axe, of course. But I've got fishnets and cutoffs. I've got black lipstick and nail polish too. I like to do the whole goth thing myself sometimes. Let me see that comic book. Can I open it?"

"Let me see your hands first. Are they clean?"

Samantha took Katy's hands and inspected them meticulously. "Okay. Just don't break the spine."

Katy flipped delicately through the comic. It was a full-sized graphic novel, just page after page of Hardcore Kelli chopping off bad guys' limbs, disemboweling them with her axe, or lopping off their heads, all while sustaining horrific injuries herself. In every other frame she was either bleeding from the nose or spitting blood. And she always seemed to have a black eye and a missing tooth. Katy couldn't help but wonder if this was how her little sister saw her.

"Who's this guy?"

On the cover, right beside Hardcore Kelli, was a tall guy in a long trench coat. He was bald and skinny, with slanted, yellow, reptilian eyes. His fingers were long and gnarled like the dried and brittle branches of a dying tree. Just looking at him made Katy want to take a shower.

"That's Creepo. He's her biggest enemy. He tortures and kills people. Kids mostly."

"Lovely. Does Mom know you read this kind of stuff?"

Samantha shrugged. "She doesn't care, as long as I'm reading."

"So, where do I get a T-shirt like that?"

"Oh, that's easy. There's a comic book shop at the mall that sells 'em. She's really popular for an indie comic book character. And I've got something else to show you, but you can't tell Mom."

Katy leaned closer and whispered. "What is it?" Whispering wasn't actually necessary. Their mother was still at work, and Katy was a grown-ass woman. Still, it felt appropriate somehow. Sharing secrets was one of the ways siblings bonded, and Katy had a lot of bonding to do to reconnect with her little sister, who was still basically a stranger.

"I've got an axe. I mean, I've got *the* axe. Hardcore Kelli's axe."

Samantha reached under her bed and slid out a big iron battle-axe that was almost as big as she was.

"I bought it from a guy at a comic book convention. It's real. It's made out of iron and steel and it can really cut!"

Katy reached down and picked up the weapon. It had to have weighed twenty or thirty pounds, and it was in fact real steel.

"Fuck! This is heavy. You got this from a guy at a comic convention?"

She ran her finger along the edge of the blade and a trickle of blood dripped down into her palm. It was sharp too. *What the hell was Samantha doing with a medieval weapon under her bed?*

"Yeah. I traded one of my best comics for it. Silver Stingray number five. That comic would be worth almost a thousand dollars now if I had kept it. But the axe is pretty cool, huh?"

Katy's mouth dropped open. *Samantha traded a thousand-dollar comic book for this? Hell, who knew there was such a thing as thousand-dollar comic books anyway?*

"Will you carry it?"

Katy smiled and rubbed her little sister's head, ruffling her bangs.

"I wouldn't be Hardcore Kelli without it, now would I? But let me ask you something. If you like her so much, why aren't *you* going as Hardcore Kelli for Halloween?"

Samantha shrugged. "Because you look more like her. I'm gonna go as a sexy vampire."

"Like hell you are!"

Samantha giggled.

"I'm serious! No sexy anything."

"Okay! Okay! I'll go as a unicorn."

Katy snickered and raised an eyebrow. "That all depends on what kind of unicorn."

"What?"

"Never mind."

"Wait—if you're going to be Hardcore Kelli, you need to study up." Samantha ran back to the closet and dragged out another shoe box.

"Here. These ones you can read. They're already all fucked up. They're not worth anything, but it will help you get in character."

She pulled out a stack of old, yellowing graphic novels, and plopped them onto Katy's lap.

"More comics?"

"Hardcore Kelli comics. Research," Samantha said, grinning proudly.

Katy picked one off the top of the stack. The cover was Hardcore Kelli engaged in a heated battle with a guy in battle armor, wearing a dark cowl.

"Who's she fighting?"

"That's Murder Man. He's a real bad dude."

Katy frowned.

"Yeah, I've known a lot of bad dudes in my time too."

"Did you kick their ass?" Samantha asked, clearly excited by the idea of her big sister beating up bad guys.

Katy's frowned deepened.

"I tried. But nobody wins every fight. Not even Hardcore Kelli."

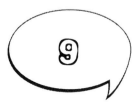

THE NEXT DAY was Halloween. Katy's mom had to leave early for work. She was a nurse at the only nearby hospital, in the next town, a two-hour drive away. She rushed past Katy but then backed up and leaned down to kiss Katy on the forehead.

"Would you make breakfast and take Samantha to school for me?"

"Sure," Katy said. "You just go on to work. I'll take care of everything."

Katy was barely awake, sitting at the kitchen table sipping coffee and trying to shake off last night's dream. It had been another doozy. Ever since she'd stopped drinking and doing drugs, the dreams had gotten worse, as had the auditory and visual hallucinations.

Her mother gathered her purse and car keys and then paused at the front door. "Samantha said you're taking her trick or treating?"

"Yeah. She asked me, and she's so damn cute I couldn't say no. I thought it would be a great way for us to bond, you know?"

Her mother nodded. There was moisture in her eyes. She let out a heavy sigh and then wiped at her eyes. "That's good. She'll like that. I'm really happy you're home."

Katy nodded. "I'm really happy to be home."

Her mother dropped her purse, ran over to the kitchen table, and scooped Katy into her arms, almost spilling Katy's coffee. "I love you, Katy."

Katy hugged her mom back. Her eyes were moist too now. "I love you too, Mom."

"Well, I'd better go. I'm going to be late," her mother said, releasing Katy from her embrace, standing, and smoothing out the wrinkles in her baby blue hospital scrubs. Tears stained her cheeks.

"Don't worry. I'll take care of Samantha."

Her mother walked back over to the front door, wiped her eyes with her sleeve, and then stooped to pick up her purse. She opened the front door and paused again.

"Katy, be careful tonight. There's going to be some kind of big Klan rally tonight."

"Klan? As in KKK?"

"Yeah."

"On Halloween? Why?"

Her mother shrugged. "Who knows. Either Obama said something to piss 'em off or Trump did something to encourage 'em. Either way, they're all fired up. So you be careful out there tonight."

Katy waved it off. "We'll be fine. We're poor white trash just like they are. I probably went to school with half of 'em."

Her mother chuckled.

"Yeah, and the other half probably went to school with me or your grandma. Still, they make me nervous. So stay away from the Wallace Ranch tonight. That's where they usually hold their rallies."

"No problem, Mom."

"Thanks again for taking Samantha. Have a great day."

"You too."

"Bye, Samantha!" her mother yelled.

"Bye, Mom!" Samantha yelled back from upstairs.

"You be good and listen to your big sister!"

"I will!"

Katy watched her mother drive off, then she got up and walked over to the refrigerator, trying to decide what to make for breakfast. There was a fresh pack of bacon and half a dozen eggs in the refrigerator along with milk and fresh orange juice.

"Bacon and eggs it is."

As Katy searched for a frying pan, Samantha came bounding into the room, filled with enough energy to power a 747.

"Good morning, Katy!"

"Good morning, 'lil Sis. How do you like your eggs?"

"Over medium."

"Well, I'll try my best. Why aren't you wearing your costume?"

"It's in my backpack. Only geeks wear their costumes to school."

Katy chuckled. "Oh, right. You're much too cool for that."

"Yup. I'm in sixth grade. Wearing costumes to school is what elementary school kids do."

"I see. And you were in elementary school what? Just last year? I guess you matured a lot over the summer."

Samantha nodded. "Yup." She didn't recognize the sarcasm in her big sister's voice.

The bacon was too crisp and the eggs a little too runny, but Samantha never complained. She ate it all quickly, drank her milk, and then launched into a fresh round of questions.

"How many people have you knocked out?"

"You mean in the ring?"

"Anywhere."

Katy thought about the walrus she'd beaten up in the club and the construction worker she'd killed in the parking lot.

"A lot. I can't remember."

"Can you teach me how to fight?"

Katy smiled. "Sure. Put your hands up."

Samantha raised her tiny fists, with her thumbs tucked inside.

"Okay. First, let me show you how to make a fist. You put your thumbs inside your hands like that and you'll break your thumbs when you hit somebody. Here, put your thumbs outside around your fingers like this."

Katy unballed Samantha's fists and then curled them up again with her thumbs out.

"Good. Now, when you hit something, you want to use these big knuckles. If you hit with the flat side of your fist, or these little knuckles, you could break your hands."

"All my knuckles are little though," Samantha said.

"Well, your bigger knuckles then. Now, I'm going to show you a one-two combination. It's the best and most basic combination. The most successful combination in boxing. It's knocked out more people than Jack Daniels."

"Who's Jack Daniels?"

"Doesn't matter. Just stand here like this with your left leg in front. Feet shoulder width apart. Knees slightly bent. When you throw your right hand, I want you to come straight down the middle. You need to put all your weight behind the punch if you want to knock someone out, so I want you to turn your shoulders and hips into the punch. Like this."

Katy flicked out a right cross that stopped inches from her little sister's nose.

"Okay, now you try it."

Katy opened her hands and held her palms up like focus mitts. Samantha began bouncing on her toes, and throwing jabs and right crosses at Katy's hands.

"Good. Good. That's it. Remember to keep your chin tucked, and turn your shoulders and hips into the punches."

Her little sister's punches landed with little smacking sounds as they struck Katy's palms. Katy began to wince with each blow. The sound of Samantha's bare fist striking skin was different than the sound a boxing glove makes when it hits you. Katy was familiar with this sound too though. She'd heard it many times before.

As she watched Samantha bounce up and down, throwing that jab and right cross combination she'd just taught her, over and over again, the little girl's features began to warp and shift, growing bigger, harder, meaner.

Smack!

A square jaw and a five-o'clock shadow took the place of her baby sister's pudgy, dimpled cheeks.

Smack!

Her beautiful blue eyes were replaced by a sallow light brown with thick red capillaries turning the whites a reddish pink. He was drunk again. He always got mean when he was drunk.

Smack!

Her tiny shoulders and arms thickened with hard, wiry muscles as they drew back for another punch.

"NOOOooo!"

SMACK!

But Katy struck first. She threw a hard uppercut to Samantha's solar plexus that doubled the little girl over and dropped her to the vinyl floor. A left hook, thrown with every ounce of strength Katy possessed, sailed over her baby sister's head. If the uppercut to her gut hadn't dropped her, that left hook just might have killed her.

Samantha sucked in a deep breath and let out a wail of pain. Katy was kneeling over her, fist raised, poised to deliver another blow, when her sister's terrified, anguished sobbing finally snapped Katy out of her delirium.

"Oh my God! What did I do? I'm so sorry. I—I didn't mean to. I—I'm so sorry."

Katy reached out for Samantha, but the little girl flinched, recoiling in horror. Tears filled Katy's eyes too now.

"Please forgive me. I didn't mean to hurt you. I'm so sorry."

This time, when Katy reached for her, Samantha allowed herself to be hugged.

"I'm so sorry. Please forgive me. I'm sorry. Are you all right?"

Samantha nodded, wiping tears from her eyes.

THEY HAD TALKED a lot on the walk to school. Katy told her little sister a little bit about how she'd been abused, and how she sometimes has flashbacks.

"I guess, you throwing punches must have triggered one."

"I'm sorry."

"Oh, you don't apologize to me. It wasn't your fault. I hurt you, remember? How's your belly?"

"It still hurts, but not too bad."

"Think some ice cream might help?"

"Hell yeah!" Samantha replied.

Katy stopped at a nearby gas station and bought a pint of mint chocolate chip. The two of them sat on a bench in the school playground eating ice cream until the bell rang, until Katy was certain she'd repaired whatever damage she'd caused.

"We still on for trick or treating tonight?"

"Yup. You're still gonna go as Hardcore Kelli, right?"

"Absolutely. Who else would I be?"

"Badass!"

Samantha gave Katy a big hug and then rushed into the building.

Katy spent the day in her pajamas, sipping instant coffee, eating Pop-Tarts, celery, and pork rinds, smoking Camel Lights, sending out resumes, waiting for the phone to ring, and reading comic books, lots and lots of comic books. She'd read through the entire stack Samantha had left for her.

After lunch, she took a walk over to the new strip mall to begin piecing together her costume for the night. She had friends who were into cosplay, went to all those crazy conventions and shit. She wished she'd kept in touch with them. They would know exactly how to help her build her costume.

It shouldn't be too hard. All I need is to find one of those T-shirts. I got this, Katy thought. And sure enough, she found three different stores that carried Hardcore Kelli T-shirts. Katy wondered how the character could have been so popular, but yet she had never heard of her before yesterday. How many times had she passed that T-shirt in a store, with that angry little face on it, and didn't even notice it?

At three o'clock, Katy began to get ready. She put on white foundation and false eyelashes with lots of mascara. Then she added black eye shadow and a smudge of dark rouge for her cheeks. She painted her nails black, then selected a lipstick color that had the melodramatic name "Raven's Wing," which basically just meant black.

Katy slipped on the T-shirt, the fishnets, the black shorts she'd cut off this morning to make even shorter, and a pair of combat boots. Finally, she picked up the axe and turned to look at herself in the mirror.

"Okay, yeah. I guess I do look pretty badass."

Katy checked her watch. It was almost four. Samantha should have been home thirty or forty minutes ago.

"Where the hell is she?"

She wondered if Samantha had forgotten all about asking Katy to go with her and had gone trick or treating with her friends right after school. Maybe she was upset about what happened at breakfast, when Katy had lost control? Maybe she was scared, scared to be alone with her violent lunatic sister?

Katy looked at herself in the mirror again, and this time all she saw was a fool in a cheap costume that made her look like an emo streetwalker. She had actually been looking forward to taking her little sister trick or treating, doing something for someone else for a change, getting to finally act like a real big sister.

Come on, kid. Don't do this to me. Come home. Don't forget about me.

When the doorbell rang, Katy knew something was wrong. Samantha wouldn't have rung the bell. She had her own key.

There were two police officers standing on the front porch, and Samantha wasn't with them. Katy felt the room shrink and the air thicken. The walk to the front door seemed to take hours, hours in which she imagined every horrible thing that could possibly befall a pretty young girl on her way home from school in a shitty neighborhood like this.

"Good Afternoon, ma'am. Are you Samantha Knox's guardian?"

"Yeah, kinda. I'm her older sister. Is she in trouble?"

"Is Samantha at home?"

"No, she's late getting home from school."

The two officers looked at each other.

"What's happened to her?"

"Well, we don't really know. We got a report from one of the kids that walks home with her, one of your neighbors, that Samantha was picked up off the street by a man in a red sports car with black rims and dark tinted windows. Do you know who that might have been? Do you have a friend or family member who drives a red sports car who might have had a reason to pick her up from school?"

Katy slowly shook her head. She felt like she was sinking beneath the ocean and the rest of the officer's questions were rolling over her like waves. She was conscious of responding, but it was all automatic, subconscious. She answered their questions and half-listened to their instructions and assurances. At some point they called her mother and told her the bad news. Katy heard her mother scream from the other end of the phone.

"You stay here in case she comes back. We're going to go talk to your neighbors to see if anyone might have seen her."

Katy nodded, still not hearing half of what was being said to her. When the police finally left, Katy stood in the entryway, staring at the front door. She could hear the squeals of laughter from kids getting an early start on trick or treating. Out the side windows, she saw costumes drift by along the sidewalk, werewolves, vampires, witches, ghosts, and superheroes. *I'm a superhero too,* Katy thought. She had to save Samantha. Katy picked up the huge battle-axe and walked out the door to look for her sister.

The sun was setting, and taking its own sweet time about it. Long shadows dragged out into the streets, and candy-gobbling ghosts and ghouls cavorted between them, racing from door to door.

"Hardcore Kelli! Great costume!"

"Oooh! Look, Mom! It's Hardcore Kelli! Are you really her?"

Katy ignored them all. She had to find her sister. She retraced the path from the house to the schoolyard. She had walked back and forth twice and was on her third trip to the school when she spotted a red sports car near the playground on the other side of the school, black rims, limo tinted windows. She took off in a sprint, gripping the axe in two hands like a hockey player charging the goalie. As she drew closer, Katy heard a scream come from within the vehicle.

"Samantha!"

Katy took the last few steps in giant leaps that launched her into the air like an Olympic long jumper. She raised the axe above her head, heedless of its weight and swung it down on the vehicle's windshield, shattering it. She heard Samantha scream again, and call out her name.

"Katy, help!"

The driver's side door opened and a man stepped out wearing a long dark trench coat. His skin was a bluish black with thick veins running like vines over a tree, bulging beneath the surface of his skin. He was nearly seven feet tall and bald. His narrow eyes glowed a sickly bile yellow, and when he smiled, his teeth were like tiny needles, lined up neatly from one corner of his mouth to the other.

"Creepo," Katy whispered, but it couldn't be. He was just a comic-book character. He wasn't real. But this was obviously not a costume. She was looking at the real deal, and he had her little sister.

"He tortures and kills people. Kids mostly…"

Not my sister.

Katy wrenched the axe free of the windshield. Creepo let out a little giggle, more of a high-pitched titter, like a man doing a falsetto impersonation of a little girl's laugh. He swatted at her with his long fingernails that were painted with a glittering purple and black nail polish. Katy felt fire sear through her calf as Creepo's nails sliced effortlessly through her flesh.

Jesus Christ that hurt!

Katy swung the axe at his skull, but he ducked and the blade swooshed harmlessly inches above his head.

"It's not going to be that easy sweetheart," Creepo taunted in that disturbing falsetto. As he moved toward her, preparing to slash at her again, Creepo's trench coat fell open revealing that he was completely naked beneath the coat, and that he had perfectly round breasts in addition to a penis. Katy wondered if he looked the same way in the comic book. *Were comics this graphic nowadays?* It wouldn't surprise her. Sex and violence was everywhere, she thought, taking a moment to consider the irony of a former stripper and borderline prostitute tsk-tsking the decline of social morality.

Creepo scampered up onto the car after Katy and she swung the axe at him again; this time it sliced his forearm open as he tried to shield his face from the blow. Inky black blood sprayed the hood of the car.

"Run, Samantha!" Katy yelled.

"I can't! He tied me up!"

This twisted, perverted thing had tied up her little sister, preparing to do who knows what to her. He deserved to die! Katy kicked the monstrous thing in one of his perfectly shaped tits, knocking him from the car hood onto his back, and then she jumped down off the car, landing on top of him with both feet in his midsection. Air exploded from Creepo's lungs and he let out a long wheeze. Katy raised the axe. It felt like it weighed a thousand pounds. She was just about to bring it down on Creepo's skull when she felt pain in her other calf and heard something go crunch! Creepo had bitten her with those little needle teeth. Pain fired through her system as Creepo thrashed his head back and forth like a shark in a feeding frenzy, lacerating muscle and skin. Katy used the butt of the axe, pounding against the thing's forehead until he finally let go of her.

When Creepo released his grip on her leg, he shoved Katy off and she toppled over onto the asphalt. She lost her grip on the axe and it clattered onto the street.

Creepo was on all fours, scampering toward her with his trench coat flapping in the air behind him like the wings of some enormous black beetle, grinning at her with that needle-toothed rictus.

"You are delishiooooouuuus!" he cooed, coming to take another piece of her. He mounted her and began slashing and biting, tearing her apart. Katy had never felt so much pain, not even in the ring when she had fought for a title, going round after round with an opponent whose speed, power and skill dwarfed her own. She had gotten pummeled then and she was getting pulverized now, ripped into glistening streams of dripping red confetti. Much of what had been inside of her, was laid out on the asphalt all around her. Creepo finally grew tired of unmaking her and turned back to his vehicle, back to Samantha. Katy couldn't save her. She had failed. She wasn't Hardcore Kelli after all. She was just a helpless piece of street trash. An imposter. A loser. And she was about to watch her little sister die.

"No. NOOOOO!!!"

Katy didn't know where she found the strength, but she somehow managed to struggle to her feet and pick up her axe. "Get the fuck away from her, you freak!"

Creepo turned back toward Katy just as she swung the axe. She saw the look of surprise on his face as the blade caught him just under the chin and sliced clean through, separating his head from his shoulders. His head clattered to the street, those yellow eyes still glowing in the twilight.

"Samantha? You okay?"

Katy staggered over to the car and yanked open the passenger side door, bracing herself for what she might see. But Samantha was okay. She was scared, tied up with bungee cords from her ankles to her shoulders, but she wasn't bleeding anywhere, and she still had all of her clothes on. Katy used the axe to cut her free.

"You did it! You did it! I told you, you made a great Hardcore Kelli. I told you she was one of the good guys. You cut his head clean off! See, sometimes heroes do kill the bad guys."

"I'm not a hero," Katy said in an exhausted rasp.

Samantha hugged her sister, nodding emphatically. "Uh huh. You are a hero. You saved my life. He was going to kill me."

"What the hell was that thing?"

Samantha shrugged. "I don't know. He was just some crack head."

"A crack head? No way, that was Creepo," Katy said.

Samantha frowned. "That's not Creepo. That's just some sick asshole."

Katy looked back over at the thing that had attacked her and her sister, at the decapitated body of an emaciated man in an old

trench coat, eyes yellowed from smoking rock cocaine, teeth broken and jagged, thick black nails grown long from neglect. Just a crack head like Samantha said. Katy had been right the first time; only psychos go around decapitating people. Only crazy people chop other people up with axes. Katy looked down at her chest and stomach where Creepo had torn her open and there were just a few shallow scratches, some deeper than others, a lot of blood, but not much damage.

"Is there still time to go trick or treating?" Samantha asked. The resiliency of children was amazing.

Katy nodded. "I think there's time. Let's go."

Katy helped Samantha out of the car.

"Tell me about Hardcore Kelli's other enemies."

"Oh. Well there's a whole Legion of Evil!"

"Legion of Evil? Sooounds kinda corny."

"No, they're really bad dudes! There's Evilene. She's an evil witch. There's Doctor Maniac, Snake-head, The Cutter, The Whisperer, The Pusher. Oooh, and Murder Man. He's Hardcore Kelli's greatest adversary. Then there's The Poison Preacher, and—"

Samantha continued to run off names of sinister bad guys, all determined to wreak havoc on Hardcore Kelli and those she loved. Katy slung the axe onto her shoulder and took her little sister by the hand. It was going to be a long night.

"Tell me more about Murder Man," Katy asked as they walked down the dark streets. Katy caught glimpses of dark, faceless shadow people darting past in her peripheral vision. She knew she was beginning to lose her grip on reality. She tightened her grip on the axe.

"Here," Samantha replied, kneeling down to dig through her

school backpack. She retrieved three comic books. All of them were of Hardcore Kelli. She pointed to a guy on the cover of one comic who wore a black cape with a hood. Under the cape he wore some sort of mechanical exoskeleton.

"He's a cyborg assassin. He has guns that come out of his forearms. And his eyes are laser sights."

Katy nodded solemnly. She knelt down and studied the picture on the cover. She flipped through the comic until she found a frame that showed Murder Man's face close up. It reminded her of someone, a memory from her childhood. Someone who'd scared her really bad once. Someone who'd hurt her once.

"He looks like someone I know," Katy said.

"He looks like Mr. Black," Samantha said.

"Who?"

"Mr. Black. The guy who runs the junkyard. Well, not *old* Mr. Black. His son. He's just a little older than you. He used to be a football star or something. But that was a looong time ago."

Katy remembered him now. And it wasn't a good memory. They'd gone to high school together. He was older. He'd been a senior when she had just started as a freshman. She stared at the comic book and could picture Sam Black's face beneath that hood. She could picture him on top of her, hurting her. Katy pushed the memory from her mind.

"Murder Man," Katy whispered. "Come on!"

She took Samantha by the hand and started walking off toward the old junkyard.

"Where we going? I thought we were going trick or treatin'?"

"We're going to find Murder Man … and stop him."

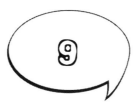

TWO FLOODLIGHTS ON motion detectors attached to the run-down trailer illuminated the front of the junkyard. A full moon set the rest of the yard aglow with pale, bluish white light. It was a necropolis of broken rusting cars, trucks, appliances, and other miscellaneous scrap metal, bed frames, bikes, gas pipes, steel beams, and even old medical equipment. The shadows here were all twisted and contorted, deformed shapes cavorting amongst the graveyard of rotting Detroit Steel. Just looking at their dark silhouettes made Katy want to scream. It was like every nightmare she'd ever had had found residence in this carnival of decay and ruin.

"You sure he lives here?" Katy asked.

Samantha nodded. "Right over there, in that trailer. He lives there with his dad."

"Fucking waste," Katy whispered.

"Hardcore Kelli calls them losers. She always calls her enemies fucking losers—or shit-stains," Samantha said.

"Can you just try to watch your language? Jesus. Does Mom know you talk like this?'

"Of course not. But you're my big sister!"

That's right. Big sister. Not a superhero. Not Hardcore Kelli. Just Samantha's big sister. Ex-boxer, ex-stripper, ex-drug-addict and alcoholic, bipolar, with a healthy dose of schizophrenia for added flavor. Which meant Sam Black wasn't Murder Man. He was just a…

"Fucking loser" seemed appropriate. Sam Black had gone from a local football hero to a thirty-one-year-old piece of shit, living with his dad in a trailer. All because the dumb fuck had flunked out of college, and lost his scholarship. Even after she'd left this town, she'd still heard stories about how he'd started partying and getting drunk every night, and stopped showing up for class or even going to practice, once word got out that he couldn't read. He'd skated through high school on his good looks and athleticism. Football had an almost canonic status in this town, so no teacher dared fail the high school's star running back. The professors at the state college had not been quite as enamored of him. Now, "Superstar" Sam Black was just one of the thousands of former high school athletes across the country, getting drunk on Friday nights and boring strangers with stories about what used to be and could have been. Katy had no pity for him. Even if he wasn't Murder Man, he was a fucking rapist. This, Katy knew firsthand.

Katy swung the axe above her head and brought it down on one of the cedar posts supporting the barbed-wire fence that surrounded the property. The dry, rotting wood post split in half and a four-foot section of the barbed wire fence came crashing down. Katy lifted Samantha over the tangle of jagged barbed wire, and together they stole their way into the junkyard.

SAMANTHA WAS NERVOUS and excited, but not frightened. She'd seen what her sister had done to the last person who'd tried to hurt her. She no longer had any doubt that her big sister Katy could protect her. But she wasn't sure exactly what they were doing in Mr. Black's junkyard. If this was supposed to be a game, or if Katy really believed that she was Hardcore Kelli, and they were about to confront Murder Man.

Some small part of Samantha accepted the possibility that her big sister Katy might really be Hardcore Kelli, and may have always been. The more she thought about it, the easier it was to accept that her sister had left home to fight crime in the big city, and Katy was just her secret identity. Didn't she hear once that most myths and legends began as true stories? What if the comic book was inspired by a real person—her big sister, Katy? There were, after all, parallels between their stories. The entire reason Samantha wanted her sister to go trick or treating as

Hardcore Kelli was because she shared so much in common with the character. They were both ex-fighters. They were both pretty buff. And they both had bad tempers. It was silly, but Samantha couldn't discount the possibility.

She scrambled over piles of trash and scrap metal, trying to keep up with her sister, and making a lot of noise doing it.

"Shhhhh! He'll hear us with all that noise you're making," Katy said, but Samantha didn't think Katy was being all that stealthy either. She was making almost as much noise as Samantha traipsing through a sea of rusting steel, copper, aluminum, and tin. There were trails carved through the piles of metal, but most of them were still covered ankle deep in rusted cans, containers, and random pieces of debris.

The junkyard was full of rats. Even if she couldn't see them, Samantha could hear them scurrying through the shadows. Not seeing them was actually worse. They could be anywhere. Everywhere. Samantha hugged her sister's leg when she heard loud squeaking and squealing, like rodents fighting. It was so dark, she wouldn't have been able to see them if there were rats scampering over her feet right now, about to scurry up her legs into her costume.

"I'm scared!"

"Shhhh!" Katy replied.

Samantha gazed up at her big sister with wide, fearful eyes. She trusted Katy. They were family. And you were always supposed to trust family. But, Samantha really didn't know her sister that well. She'd heard stories about her big sister her entire life. She'd watched Katy fight on TV, winning and losing, and she'd just seen her take down that creep who'd kidnapped her less than thirty minutes ago. But why didn't Katy call the police? Wasn't that what you were supposed to do when you killed someone? You were supposed to call the cops, and they would come and put up police tape, and draw chalk outlines around the body, and take pictures, and ask everyone a bunch of questions, and then they'd wrap up the body in a big black bag and haul it away in a van. That's how it always happened on TV. But Katy had just left the body lying in the street and walked away.

No one even knew where they were. Not even their mom. Why hadn't Katy called to tell anyone that Samantha was safe?

"Katy? Shouldn't we call Mom?"

"Don't call me that."

Samantha was struggling to keep up as they scrambled noisily through the junkyard. She was already breathing hard.

"Don't call you what?" Samantha asked.

"Katy."

"But that's your name. Katy."

"It's my secret name. My secret identity."

Samantha felt goose bumps raise on her skin. She didn't know why, but her sister was scaring her. Something wasn't right about her.

"Soooo, you're ..."

"Hardcore Kelli."

Samantha stopped walking.

"Come on. We're almost to his lair."

"Whose lair? Old Man Black's Lair? Sam Black's secret hide-out? Come on, Sis. This is make-believe, right? He's not really Murder Man. And you're not really Hardcore Kelli. We can't just run up to him and chop his head off."

When Katy stopped walking and turned to look at Samantha, the moon caught her eyes just right, so that all the madness within her shone brilliant in her face. She looked like some madcap clown, a demented jester with an axe. Moonlight glinted off the axe too. Except where it was still caked with Creepo's blood. Samantha had never seen a crazy person before, but she knew then that she was looking at one.

"We'll do whatever it takes to stop Murder Man for good."

"I want to go home," Samantha said.

"Shhhh!"

"I'm scared! I don't want to be here!"

"Then go home!" Katy yelled, turning to face Samantha again, this time gripping the axe in a way that made Samantha feel even more terrified, even more certain that Katy wasn't completely sane. Because there were only two possibilities that Samantha could see, either her sister was out of her mind, or she really was a superhero, and Sam Black really was some sort of supervillain, and that just wasn't possible.

Was it?

Katy turned and walked away. "I'm telling Mom!" Samantha yelled, and then she began to run, tripping over debris as she made her way back to the fence her sister had knocked down. By the time she reached it, she had cuts and bruises on her arms and legs from banging into things in the dark and falling over and into the piles of scrap metal. She looked back toward the trailer where Sam Black lived, in the direction her sister had been going. She saw the door of the trailer open, and Sam step out carrying some sort of rifle. He was wearing a sweatshirt with a hood, and in the distance, he did look a lot like Murder Man.

"Who's out there? You better get off my property if you don't want to get shot!"

She saw her sister step out of the shadows into the light, hefting the axe in her hands.

"You aren't shooting anybody, Murder Man. Your reign of terror is over!" Katy yelled back. Then she raised the axe, and charged...

And Murder Man opened fire.

"Katy, no!"

Samantha started to run back into the junkyard, but she knew there was nothing she could do to help. She was just a kid, and she was unarmed. If she ran back in there to save her sister, they would both get shot. So, instead, she turned and ran back down the dark, lonely, road they had come. Past houses decorated with glowing skeletons and jack-o'-lanterns, mummies, vampires, and witches on broomsticks. She ran past Styrofoam tombstones and inflatable Frankenstein monsters, weaving her way between kids dressed as monsters, demons, Disney characters, and superheroes. She had run for three blocks, but she could still hear the gunshots. Tears splayed across her face as the wind kicked up, making the trees sway and moan and jack-o'-lanterns flicker. This time she hoped her sister really was a superhero, not because she thought it would be cool to have the real Hardcore Kelli as a sibling, but because that was the only way she could imagine Katy surviving.

MURDER MAN. THAT'S what she'd called him.

How the fuck did she know?

Sam didn't have a clue how this crazy chick in the Halloween costume had found out about his little hobby, but she was trespassing on his property, threatening him with an axe, and that meant he was well within his rights, as a taxpaying citizen of these United States, to shoot her down where she stood.

"I'm giving you one last chance to get off my property, or I'm gonna shoot you full of holes! You hear me?"

"I'm not going nowhere, Murder Man. I'm taking you down!"

There was something weird about how she was talking. It sounded like lines from a movie or something. Sam looked around, wondering if maybe someone was playing a prank on him. He half expected to see Jake or Larry from the saloon hiding behind one of those rusted old cars with a video camera. But that didn't make sense either. They would have revealed themselves the minute he began shooting. No one would take a joke this far and risk getting themselves killed. And then there was that name she kept calling him.

Murder Man.

"Why do you keep calling me that?" Sam yelled, still firing, and hitting nothing.

"Because that's who you are! A killer. An assassin. And that's why you have to be stopped," the girl with the axe said, still coming forward.

There was no doubt about it now. She knew about him somehow, and that meant he couldn't let her leave. He had to end her. But what if she'd already told someone? What if she had friends? Family? Someone who knew where she was, and why? They would know something was wrong if she disappeared. That would mean cops would come sniffing around, so he would have to do some quick tidying up. But Sam had been preparing for just such an eventuality ever since he'd taken up his little hobby. The shed out back where he kept his friends sat on a trailer that he could haul off somewhere safe before he called the police to report shooting a trespasser who'd come onto his property, talking crazy and swinging an axe. The rest of the house was clean. He never played with his friends in the house. You don't shit where you eat.

"Stand still, you crazy bitch!"

The AR-15 bucked in his hands, spraying bullets wildly. Between the recoil and his own agitated breathing, Sam was sending bullets high and low, hitting nothing but dirt and sky. And the crazy bitch was getting closer. He needed to calm himself down, take his time, and aim.

Sam took his finger off the trigger, took a deep breath, and lined up the sights. At first, he saw nothing but darkness, but then he saw her dart past his sights. He squeezed the trigger, but she was already gone. The crazy chick was zigzagging as she ran. It was hard enough to hit a moving target in the dark, but hitting one that wasn't moving in a straight line was almost impossible. Especially after polishing off a twelve pack of Pabst Blue Ribbon. He was lucky he hadn't shot himself yet. And Sam hadn't brought an extra magazine with him. The rest of his ammo was still in the house, and Sam wasn't sure how many bullets he'd already wasted. He had a thirty-round clip, so he knew he wasn't out yet, but he couldn't afford to waste many more. And all the noise he was making would bring the police before he'd had a chance to hide his friends. He needed to wait until she was closer.

Maybe he could just wound her, take her out back to the shed with the rest of his friends. She wasn't bad looking. She was slender, and had a nice pair of tits flopping around beneath her T-shirt. He could have a lot of fun with her before she bled to death. He might even be able to stop the bleeding and keep her alive for a few days. Thinking up a story to tell the cops if they showed up wouldn't be too hard, even in Sam's current state of inebriation. It wouldn't be hard for them to believe he'd just gotten drunk and decided to shoot rats in the junkyard. If she bled a lot, he'd have to shoot one of his dogs and lay its body where she'd fallen. A crazy redneck getting drunk and shooting his own dog would just make a funny story for the cops to tell down at The Saloon. No one would find it the least bit suspicious.

The crazy chick leapt up onto the porch, swinging the big axe, trying to chop Sam in half. She had gotten much closer than he had intended. Close enough that he felt the "whoosh!" as the axe sailed past just inches from his forehead. Sam jerked backward, startled, but managed to put one bullet in her thigh and another in her abdomen. She crumpled to the ground like a deflated blow-up doll. Sam tried to kick the axe out of her hands, but she held on, snarling at him with eyes that radiated hatred.

"Oh, you're a tough one, ain't ya? It's going to be fun breaking you. I'll find out just how tough you really are."

Sam raised his rifle and brought the butt of it down on the girl's forehead. Then he reached down and snatched the axe from her hands.

"Yeah, we'll see how tough you are. We're going to have lots of fun, you and me."

The shed where Sam kept his "friends" was about two hundred yards from the house. The woman in black with the dark makeup lay curled up at Sam's feet in a fetal position. She was small, but it was still going to be a bitch carrying her that far. He didn't have a choice though. He had little doubt that cops would be coming soon. Everyone for at least a mile or two had to have heard the gunshots. If he was lucky, they would assume it was just some kids playing a Halloween prank. Still, the crotchety old fucks around here wouldn't hesitate to call the police on a bunch of harmless kids having a laugh. They had nothing better to do with their miserable lives than to ruin other people's fun, and that included Sam's. Besides, he hadn't avoided police scrutiny this long relying on luck. It was better to stick with his original plan. Get this crazy chick inside the shed, hook the shed to his truck, and drag it the hell out of here.

The woman was only barely conscious. That blow to her skull with the butt of his rifle had taken away whatever fight inside her the bullet in her gut hadn't. She laid in a pool of her own blood, eyes closed, holding her gut and moaning.

"Come on, girlie. Let's get you up."

Sam reached down and grabbed the woman by her arms, pulling her up to a sitting position. He took off his belt and used it to bind her wrists. It wasn't the best way to bind her, especially with her hands and wrists slippery with her own blood, but it would be good enough to restrain her until he could get her into the shed where he had other ways to immobilize her. She cried out in pain when Sam knelt down and wrapped his arms around her waist, lifting the bleeding woman onto his shoulders in a fireman's carry. She struggled feebly, kicking and bucking, before going limp; shock and blood loss had rendered her helpless, just like Sam liked them.

Sam smiled and licked his tobacco-stained teeth. He didn't know who this crazy chick was, or why she was here, but he was going to find out. Interrogation scenes were his favorite. One way or another, he'd discover who she was, where she lived, how she knew about him, and who that other voice belonged to that he was certain he'd heard out in his yard when he first started shooting. Grunting under the strain of her weight, Sam began walking toward the metal shed.

"Goddamn, this bitch is heavy," Sam grumbled.

After what felt to him like a full five minutes, Sam reached the shed. He lowered the woman to the ground and fished in his pocket for the keys to the big, heavy padlock on the door. He could already hear the girls inside crying and whimpering.

"Nooo! Pleeease, noooo! No more!"

"What did I tell you whores about getting loud? Do you need a reminder of what happens when you disobey me?"

Sam whipped open the door to the shed and smiled when he saw his friends.

I T WAS HARD to keep her eyes open. Katy felt like just drifting off to sleep. But the putrescent stench that wafted from that little metal shed when Murder Man opened it was like smelling salts. It jarred Katy out of her stupor. The sight that assailed her senses beyond the shed door, illuminated by the silver glow of the full moon, was even worse than the smell.

Bodies, both alive and dead, all chained together. Some had already begun to rot. Bloated, leaking fluids, mottled skin sloughing off as the women who were still alive rubbed against them. As if Murder Man couldn't be bothered with disposing of bodies, so he'd just kept shoving new girls in there on top of the dead ones. Stacked on top of each other, floor to ceiling, like a human compost heap. All girls. All young. Twenty-somethings. Teenagers. Some younger. Most of them were Mexican. Some black. One or two white ones. Migrant workers, runaways, prostitutes, homeless kids. Easy prey. Girls no one would be looking for, in a place no one would look, where no one would notice the smell of death.

They had clearly been beaten. Probably raped. Quite a few of them had cigarette burns on their arms and legs. Some of the dead ones had dark bruises around their necks. Strangled. Others had likely suffocated under the crush of other bodies. Some of the living girls had clawed their way free of the dead, literally digging through a hill of putrefying flesh in search of fresh air and room to breathe. Fetid blood and organs formed a thick stew of rot and decay at the bottom of the shed. And Murder Man intended to toss Katy right in there with them, into that rancid abattoir.

He swatted away the clutching hands of a young Mexican woman with a black eye and swollen lip, reaching out for him out of that pile of rotting flesh, and grasped the arm of a freshly dead black woman who had not yet begun to rot. Locked onto the dead woman's wrist was a metal shackle affixed to a thick iron chain. There was another cuff attached to the opposite end of the chain, and Murder Man lifted the empty shackle, then used a dirty handkerchief to wipe away a smear of some unknown bodily fluids before shoving the handkerchief back in his pocket and turning toward Katy.

Katy wanted to scream. Hardcore Kelli, however, wanted to kill. This piece of shit loser needed his ass kicked. But she hadn't healed yet. She was still wounded, still losing blood. If only she still had her axe.

That face she'd seen in her nightmares so many times, looked at her without recognition. He reached down to lift her again, but this time, Kelli/Katy was ready for a fight. She easily slipped her blood-slicked hands out of the belt looped around her wrists.

HARDCORE KELLI

Just as Murder Man's face reached her eye level, Katy swung a left hook at his jaw, her best left hook, the one her former trainer, Taco, had called "One of the best left hooks in all of boxing," the one that should have won her a world title and kept her from ever returning to this shit-hole town.

It connected solidly with Murder Man's jaw. Hardcore Kelli felt the impact from her fist all the way to her shoulders. It was a good punch. A great punch. Murder Man wobbled and fell backward through the door of the shed.

The pain from the gunshot wound disappeared as adrenaline and endorphins raced through her bloodstream. This man had tried to hurt her—again. He'd hurt all those women. He'd murdered so many. He had to be brought to justice. He had to be stopped. Years ago, Katy had been too weak to fight back. And maybe she still was. But Hardcore Kelli wasn't.

"Help us! Please help us! Let us go!" the women in the shed called out. At least the ones not already dead or traumatized into silence.

Hardcore Kelli rose from the floor. They needed her help, and that's what heroes did. They helped the weak and innocent. Hardcore Kelli was neither weak nor innocent. What she was, was pissed off.

LEAPING THROUGH THE doorway, Hardcore Kelli spotted Murder Man attempting to stagger to his feet. Blood gushed from his busted nose, which was twisted crooked on his face. He'd fallen into the pile of human flesh he'd crammed into the shed, and was slipping in the blood, excrement, and necrotic fluids that coated the floor. Half a dozen hands reached out, scratching, grabbing, and clawing at him, restraining him.

"No! Get off me! Get the fuck off me!" Murder Man yelled, trying his best to free himself from the tangle of limbs.

Hardcore Kelli smiled. "It's over, Murder Man." There was no need to restrain herself. No need to worry about accidentally killing someone. Killing Murder Man was exactly what she intended to do.

She threw the same uppercut to the solar plexus—left hook to the jaw combination she'd almost hit Samantha with earlier. This time, the left hook connected before Murder Man doubled over from the force of the gut punch. His victims were holding him up, keeping him on his feet so he could take more punishment. He was a living punching bag as Hardcore Kelli doubled her left hook, throwing one to the rib cage, and another to the jaw that whipped his head sideways and knocked him unconscious. She dug a right hook to Murder Man's rib cage, followed by a left uppercut to the chin that seemed to wake him up again. His eyes opened momentarily, then rolled back in his head as Hardcore Kelli rained down hooks and straight rights at his exposed face.

His face was a ruin. Bruised, swollen, and bleeding. It was almost unrecognizable. He hung limply from the women's hands as they scratched and clawed at him, trying to do as much additional damage as they could to the man who had caused them so much pain.

HARDCORE KELLI TURNED and walked out of the shed, back toward the house.

"Wait! Let us go! Don't leave us! Hellllp!" The women called out from behind her as she weaved and stumbled her way back to the main house, fighting both exhaustion and blood loss. She retrieved her axe from the porch where Murder Man had dropped it and walked back to the shed, dragging the axe behind her. In the distance, she could hear the wail of sirens. They merged with the cries of Murder Man's victims into one long, mournful dirge.

"I'm coming. I'll save you," she whispered, struggling to remain conscious.

Murder Man was still unconscious when Hardcore Kelli made it back to the shed. The women had released him, and he had tumbled into the tacky, coagulating pool of rotting effluence coating the floor of the shed. Hardcore Kelli reached down and pushed his face down into that puddle of decay, drowning him in it, while digging through Murder Man's pockets for the key to the shackles. She tossed the keys to the girls before she raised the axe for the first swing, taking Murder Man's right leg off at the kneecap. He awoke from his stupor with a scream. Hardcore Kelli raised the axe again, this time bringing it down upon his left arm, hacking it off at the shoulder. She had no intention of making his death a quick one. No quicker than the torture and death these women had suffered. The next blow took off his right arm, the next his left foot, the next cut into his thigh. It took two more swings to cut through the femur and sever that limb as well.

Unlocking themselves one at a time, Murder Man's victims emerged from the shed, covered in rot and gore. Red and blue flashing lights lit up the junkyard. Three police cruisers charged onto the property. Doors opened, and police officers stepped out with guns drawn.

Murder Man lay convulsing on the floor, dying of shock. But Hardcore Kelli wasn't done with him yet. She raised the axe again and brought the heavy blade down the center of his torso, between chest and stomach. When she wrenched the blade free, blood and chunks of internal organs flew. His intestines boiled up out of the tremendous rupture, spilling onto the floor. When she stood over him, raising the huge battle axe above her head for the final blow, she paused, waiting until she was certain he knew it was coming, until his eyes were clear and lucid.

"Look at me!" she yelled, and he did. His eyes focused on her, and for one moment, there was recognition in them. She wasn't sure if he'd finally remembered the little freshman who'd had a crush on him more than a decade ago, who he'd lured out behind the bleachers, held down, tore off her panties, and forced himself

inside, while she'd begged and cried. The little girl he'd punched and slapped until she'd finally stopped crying and just allowed it to happen. She wondered if it was the recognition of his guilt, of karma coming back upon him, or it was just the recognition of his own imminent death. She preferred to believe he saw her, really saw her, and knew why he was about to die.

He opened his mouth to scream again, but only blood bubbled out from between his lips. Then the axe came down and split his skull in two. Murder Man was finally dead.

SAMANTHA SAT IN the back of a patrol car, staring out the window at the chaos. Naked women, covered in blood, ran screaming from a shed in Mr. Black's backyard. The cops looked confused. She had told them about her sister, and Sam Black shooting at her. But this was something completely different. They hadn't been prepared for this.

Some of the officers were busy corralling the screaming women, draping jackets over them to shield their naked bodies from the elements, and offer them some comfort and modesty. The others approached the shed with their guns drawn.

"Come out with your hands up! Get on the ground! Get down on the ground!" Samantha heard the police officers call out. Then came strangled cries of pain, gunshots, and horrible sounds like the sound of a cleaver chopping through meat. The officers who'd been helping the girls ran to assist their colleagues. More gunshots. More cries of pain. More wet, thudding, chopping sounds.

Samantha knelt in the backseat of the police vehicle, staring out the back windshield, trying to see what was going on. She saw a blood-drenched battle-axe rise, the blood glistening in the moonlight.

"No! Oh, God no! Nooooo!"

Then the axe fell once, twice, and there was silence. A woman, soaked in fresh blood from head to toe, wearing cutoff black jean shorts, torn black leggings, and the unmistakable black T-shirt with that angry white face on it, a Hardcore Kelli T-shirt, walked toward the vehicle, wobbling unsteadily, dragging the huge axe. She looked like she was ready to collapse. Behind her, almost a dozen police officers lay dead. Hacked to pieces. If it hadn't been for the T-shirt, Samantha would not have recognized her sister through the mask of gore covering her face.

When Samantha looked at the zombie-like madwoman staggering toward her, what she saw was the person she'd seen in so many comic books and graphic novels. This was like the final frame of the story, after the battle had been won, the hero victorious. It wasn't Katy. Not anymore. It was Hardcore Kelli. There was no doubt now that she really existed. What Samantha still wondered was if Katy had ever really existed at all.

As her sister approached the police car, Samantha noticed that a sizeable chunk of her skull was missing, where a bullet had sheared it away just above her left eye. Her brain on that side was completely exposed. Several bullet holes dotted her chest and stomach. At least half a dozen. Maybe more. She staggered past, eyes wide and glassy. She glanced at Samantha, and Katy froze, afraid Hardcore Kelli might see her as an enemy, a threat, and take her out the way she'd taken out those cops. But she looked right through her without seeing her, and kept walking past, out of the junkyard, and down the road.

Samantha stepped out of the vehicle, and walked out into the street. She watched her sister walk away until she could no longer see her, until the night swallowed her up and she was gone for good.

Samantha never saw her sister again.

THE SHADOW MEN were everywhere. They had come for her, like she'd always known they would. But she had fought them. And she had won. She had killed every one of those bastards.

She didn't know where she was going now. Everything hurt. Her head was buzzing like it was full of bees, and a thudding migraine made it impossible to think. She just knew she had to keep moving. There were villains out there hurting people, hurting little girls, little girls—like Samantha? Where was Samantha? Samantha had told her their names: Evilene, Doctor Maniac, Snakehead, The Cutter, The Whisperer, The Pusher, and The Poison Preacher. The entire Legion of Evil. She'd stopped Creepo and Murder Man and his minions, but there were so many more. They had to be stopped too. They all had to be brought to justice.

She didn't know how long she'd been walking when she came upon their secret lair. The entire Legion of Evil, and it looked like they were preparing for war. Some of them wore white hoods over their heads, like ghosts, but she could still recognize them. There was no hiding from Hardcore Kelli.

On a makeshift wooden stage, surrounded by torches, The Poison Preacher stood, addressing a crowd of evildoers. She couldn't make out much of what he was saying. His words were drowned out by the buzzing in her skull. But she could tell by his inflections, by the angry shouts from the crowd, that he was preparing some fresh reign of terror.

"Not if I can stop it."

Hardcore Kelli raised her axe and ran into the crowd of white hooded villains, chopping them down where they stood, one at a time. Decapitating, dismembering, and disemboweling in a frenzy of battle-rage. She no longer felt any pain. She no longer felt any fear. All there was was the battle, the fight for justice.

The screams and cries of the evildoers was like a song. Some ran. Some were stupid enough to attack. She felt a few bullets whiz past her. A few more punched into her torso. But Hardcore Kelli kept coming. Because that's what she does, she always keeps coming. A fiery cross burned just to the left of the stage, towering above them, casting an orange glow over the pile of bodies as Hardcore Kelli waged her final battle against evil, as she turned the gathering of villains and murderers into a bloodbath.

Made in the USA
Middletown, DE
12 September 2021